THE STORY OF THE Easter Bunny

AUTHOR'S NOTE

When my son, Tyler, was about four years old, he became fascinated with the Easter Bunny. Ever inquiring, he wanted to know how the Easter Bunny came to be—how did he assume such a wonderful job? And how and where did the Easter Bunny make all the beautiful things we find in our Easter baskets every year? This is the story that answers all those questions.

This book is dedicated to Tyler,
who has always been the Easter Bunny's greatest admirer.
—K.T.

For Jonny and Katie.
—S.A.L.

Library of Congress Cataloging-in-Publication Data
Tegen, Katherine Brown.
The story of the Easter Bunny / by Katherine Tegen ; illustrated by Sally Anne Lambert.—1st ed.
p. cm.
Summary: A little rabbit watches an old couple paint eggs, make chocolate, and braid baskets for the village children at Easter, and he eventually becomes the Easter Bunny.
ISBN-10: 0-06-050711-X (trade bdg.) — ISBN-13: 978-0-06-050711-4 (trade bdg.)
ISBN-10: 0-06-050712-8 (lib. bdg.) — ISBN-13: 978-0-06-050712-1 (lib. bdg.)
ISBN-10: 0-06-058781-4 (pbk.) — ISBN-13: 978-0-06-058781-9 (pbk.)
[1. Easter—Fiction.] I. Lambert, Sally Anne, ill. II. Title.
PZ7.T22964St 2005 2003027852
[E]—dc22 CIP
AC

Typography by Jeanne L. Hogle

10 11 12 13 SCP 10 9
❖
First Edition

THE STORY OF THE
Easter Bunny

By Katherine Tegen • Illustrated by Sally Anne Lambert

HarperCollinsPublishers

On a snow-cold day
in a snug little house,
a round old couple
were making Easter eggs.

The round old man blew the insides out.
The round old woman painted designs
on some of the eggs.

The rest they dyed in glass cups,
while their little rabbit watched.

There were eggs the color of daffodils
and of soft new leaves
and of robins' eggs
and of violets.

On a day when the winter wind blew outside,
the round old couple made baskets out of straw.

They wove and twisted
and braided the straw together,
while their little rabbit watched.

On an early spring day when the snow was melting
and water trickled down the eaves,
the round old couple made chocolate eggs.

The round old woman melted the chocolate
and the sugar and the butter on the stove.
The round old man poured the chocolate into tiny molds.
And their little rabbit watched.

One day when the sky was blue
and the church bells rang
and the world seemed new,
everyone in the village said, "Happy Easter!"

The round old couple brought every child
a straw basket filled with Easter eggs,
as they did every year.
And their little rabbit watched.

A year went by, and Easter came again.

The straw baskets
were on the table . . .

the Easter eggs were in a
big bowl . . .

the chocolate eggs were carefully wrapped in foil . . .

and the round old couple were fast asleep.
But there was still work to be done.

The little rabbit twitched his nose.
Then he hopped up onto the table
and put the eggs into the baskets.

It was magic.

The little rabbit scooped up the baskets
and hopped down the lane.
He left one for every child in the village.
He didn't think anyone saw him.

The next year the little rabbit colored the eggs,

and cooked the chocolate,

and wove the baskets,

and delivered them
on Easter morning.

The little rabbit made more baskets every year.
The round old couple helped him.

The little rabbit hopped all over the countryside.
And the children knew, *The Easter Bunny came!*

One year the round old couple could not help
the little rabbit anymore.
They were so very, very old.
And the rabbit knew he could not stay
in their snug little house anymore.
Too many children were discovering his secrets.

So the little rabbit found the perfect place
to make his baskets in a shadow-filled wood nearby.
Only a rabbit could find the entrance.

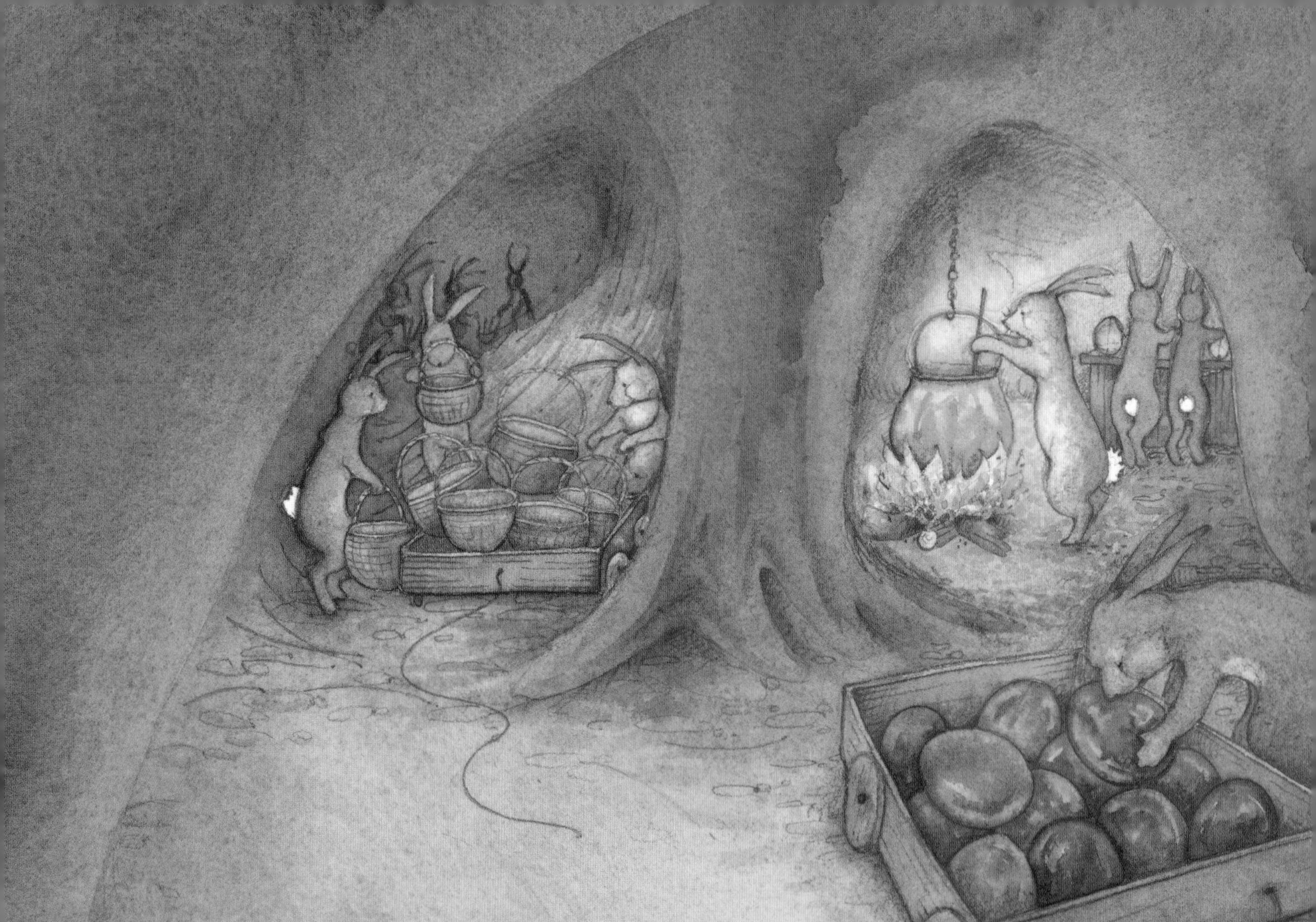

The rabbit set up one room
for making chocolate eggs,
one room for coloring eggs,
and one room for weaving baskets.
The little rabbit's friends came to help him.

Now every year on Easter morning,
when the sky is blue
and church bells ring
and the world seems new,
the Easter Bunny delivers his baskets.

Perhaps he has left one for you?

Happy Easter!